For Laura and for Emily — with gratitude

FSC
www.fsc.org
MIX
Paper from
responsible sources
FSC® C020056

First edition 2018

Library of Congress Catalog Card Number pending
ISBN 978-0-7636-9598-9

18 19 20 21 22 23 LEO 10 9 8 7 6 5 4 3 2 1

Printed in Heshan, Guangdong, China

This book was typeset in Goudy.
The illustrations were done in pen and watercolor.

Candlewick Press
99 Dover Street
Somerville, Massachusetts 02144

visit us at www.candlewick.com

CANDLEWICK PRESS

SIMON JAMES

The Boy who went to Mars

On the day Stanley's mom had to go away,
Stanley decided to leave planet Earth.
"It's just for work — I'll be back tomorrow,"
said Mom. "Be good for Dad."

"Aren't you going to wave good-bye?" said Dad.
But Stanley didn't.

Stanley ran out into the yard, climbed into his
spaceship, and blasted off into outer space . . .

heading for Mars.

A little while later, the spaceship landed back
in Stanley's yard.

A small martian crawled out.

"Hello, Stanley," said Will. "Why are you wearing
that funny hat?"
"I'm not Stanley. I'm a martian," said the martian.

"Well, you look exactly like my
brother, Stanley," said Will.

"Well, I'm not," insisted the martian.
"I've come to explore your sibilization.
Take me to your leader."

"Dad!" said Will. "I found a martian in the yard!"

"Hello, Martian," said Dad.
"You've arrived just in time for dinner.
Would you like to wash your hands?"

"I think you'll find martians
don't wash their hands,"
said the martian.
"Oh," said Dad.

At dinner, the martian wasn't impressed.
"Martians don't like Earth food," he said.
"We don't eat rocks."
"It's not a rock," said Dad. "It's a baked potato."

For dessert, Dad gave the
martian some ice cream.
"That's more like it,"
said the martian.

After dinner the martian helped clear the table.

"It's time for bed," said Dad. "Tomorrow is a school day."

"I think you'll find martians don't have bedtimes,"
said the martian.

"I think you'll find they do on Earth," said Dad.

In the bathroom, Will was getting ready for bed.
"I suppose martians don't have to brush their teeth," said Will.
"That's right," said the martian. "And we don't have to
wash either."

That night, the martian slept in Stanley's bed.
Dad came upstairs to tuck him in.
"Do martians always wear their helmets in bed?"
asked Dad.
"Always," said the martian.
"Night-night, then," said Dad.

The next day at school, the martian
met Stanley's best friend, Josh.
"You're not a martian," said Josh.

"Yes, I am," said the martian.
"You're not," said Josh. "You're Stanley!"
"Am not!" said the martian.
"You are!" insisted Josh.

The martian was upset.
He pushed Josh away!

Josh burst into tears and
ran off to tell the teacher.

After saying sorry to Josh, the martian spent the rest
of the morning sitting outside the principal's office
thinking about his behavior.

"Miss Cosmos told me what happened today,"
said Dad on the way home from school.
The martian was silent.
"I wonder what Mom will think when she gets
home tonight," said Dad.

That evening, Will and the
martian heard the front door
open and raced downstairs.

"Mom!" said Will. "We missed you!"

"I missed you, too," said Mom. "What have you been up to?"

"Well, we've had a martian living with us," said Will.
"Look, here he is!"

"Hello there," said Mom. "Have you
been a good little martian?"

The little martian froze. He didn't know what to say.
Suddenly, he turned and ran.

Out in the yard, he climbed into his spaceship
and blasted off into outer space . . .

heading back to Mars.

Moments later, the spaceship landed back on Earth.

Out peered
an Earth boy
named Stanley.

He ran up the
steps and into
the kitchen.

"Mom, I've just gotten back from Mars! You wouldn't believe it," said Stanley. "They never wash or eat their vegetables, and they're always in trouble at school!"

"Well, I'm glad you're back," said Mom. "I missed you!"

"Me too," said Stanley. "Me too."